T0123232

Also by Kasey C. Jones

Handcrafted
Outgo

A Collection of Poems

KASEY C. JONES

authorHOUSE®

AuthorHouse™
1663 Liberty Drive
Bloomington, IN 47403
www.authorhouse.com
Phone: 833-262-8899

Published by AuthorHouse 07/13/2022

Library of Congress Control Number: 2022913109
ISBN: 978-1-6655-6483-0 (sc)
ISBN: 978-1-6655-6482-3 (e)

Print information available on the last page.

This book is printed on acid-free paper.

Dedicated to Pete and Chasten
and Lia and Jazz and all allies.

Contents

Introduction

I feel that some of these poems are presenting storytelling, elegance, a matter of fact, a matter of fiction. This is what Kasey is known for, forgive me for saying that the flavors are so delicious. The elements so varied yet distinct.

Jones at times opts for simple and bold explanations that is meant to capture readers from diverse reading levels and yet maintain sophistication and clarity. Jones often attributes this quality to his love of poets such as Maya Angelou and Brenna Twohy to name just two.

Jones of course, hopes that readers will take away greater knowledge and or a broader understanding of what our fellow humans may experience, and bring closer a joyful meaning to life.

I Awake

I awake with the fresh white covering all over me. The sheet is light. I quickly get ready for the day in the bathroom. I go outside, drive a few blocks, its lunch time and I spot one of my favorite places to eat at. My food is visible on a flat tray exposing everything to my delight. The waitress gave me a depressing look as if she was having a bad day. Even her tone was raunchy and fast. I felt somewhat slighted that I had to experience such rudeness. I had no clue why this waitress was allowing our day to be turned blue.

Great Accommodations

Traveling on a bus as I blow off a little steam because my trip to see my son, will not be effortless. Some random, cute guy likes me as he rolls some assorted candies in paper towels. He leaves it where I could find it, such a flirt. He also leaves me compliments on my appearance and how he enjoys my diplomatic spirit. It does not hurt that he is also the driver of the bus and has been dragging us exhausted passengers down never-ending legs of cement. At one point, when I came back from lunch, he had put the rolled-up paper towels in my seat, how smart. Ironically, all the main accommodations were also pleasing. As you might can tell, I am not fond of busses but at least today I could sleep well.

The Creams

The creams I touched, valid; the fires, the lavenders, there were others and cool breezes. The amber oil, (over my hair) given to me by my splendid Aunt. Radiating the love of all my aunts and how they are all a different shade of pink, purple or blue. I remember one of them listening to Lauryn Hill, you know the song with the Supremes hairstyles. She was dropping us off at the Boys and Girls Club, my, that pool looked so tempting but of course we all had a type of cream in our hair, and we silently decided to just watch the other kids. Oh, and the sun the shifting trees: medium green and stale-like dark brown.

Kasey C. Jones

In the Ocean

I'm in the Ocean. I am staring the whale in the eye.

I'm in an enormous school room assigned for group trials.

I am interested in learning more about LGBTQ life and pride.

I am generally in discussions about queer families, jobs and boundaries.

In the Ocean, I am welcoming to all communities as I realize we are all over the world. Some of us are blind to our own colors, some of us are blind to each other. The whale is always around, and we feel we will always see it.

Mrs. Flannigan

Hello, Mrs. Flannigan you were a worker at one of the facilities I was admitted to. I am sure you took pride in your job, I am sure you were somebody's grandmother. I am sure that by now you would not even remember me. Would you care to know that I have a Tiktok character private on my channel that I call Mrs. Flannigan and she is appropriately named after you with my added tweaks and dramatizations. If there is anything I could thank you for now, it would be your kind personality, your dedication and for goodness' sake those orange fingernails. I also would tell you that I too have found a sense of pride in being myself one hundred percent. I will never forget you, while I was likely one of your many clients. You worked at Walter Reed Army Medical Center before they moved. After that I don't know what you did.

Kasey C. Jones

You and Me, Broken on my Good Teeth

I love it, speaking of these golden pancakes, three for me
Because I'm good and starving.
I am living it up, smiling, putting these golden pancakes
In my mouth, three pieces at a time, plate devoured.
They were hot, hanging on my fork,
Broken on my good teeth and says,
You and me every day forever babe.

She'll Say it Better

Like, why must we pay to live on a planet we were born on? This presents a problem for homeless people, who are just as valued as you and me because no one is inferior really. I know you must be sick and tired of seeing panhandlers, but your course of action is to simply raise housing costs.

Like, we should forget the outdated constitution for many people cannot be trusted with guns, leading me to think that they should be abolished completely. However, it is also your decision of course.

Like, why do we need a faulty system in place telling us when we have reached our desired education levels.

Like, why.

The Real Kasey C. Jones

I am sharp as the beggar's cheese.
The defensiveness begins after
you hear my voice so rich and fun.
If you are the blue vase, then so
am I, mellow and nourishing
around and far. One day I hold,
time and watch through the window's
bland jacket of which I cannot
cut.
I am at a short distance wave.
The calculated me I note,
with surety you have met me.
If I am a pair of glasses,
then you could be a glass of half-
emptied water nourishing just
one person through some window's
Bland jacket of which you now know.
May.

It Got All Over the Floor

The it being aliens.
Finally, we are at the cockpit.
However, I am not a plane.
I am an UFO and less toxic
these days, should I come on in.
My skin is not green or purple.
My eyes don't protrude outward.
My voice does not scare you honey.
My diet is as tame as yours.

Kasey C. Jones

I Am Not Kidding

I am thinking just above
the average, who me yes, I am just
thinking with creativity.
I am thinking along the lines of
Alice Walker, Sarah Kay.
I am not kidding sleeping beds, I
creep into art on umbrellas.
I am thinking that I am thirsty,
and you laugh at my empty bed.

For the Win

And I think of Nikita Gill using words so brilliantly laid, so effortlessly picked and shined.

And I think of Maya Angelou amongst the wind possibly helping us in.

And I think of Amiri Baraka giving us questions and history to ponder come light.

And I think of Brenna Twohy styling our clothes with messages for home.

And I think of Langston Hughes begging our guides to ensure a good word night.

And I think of Edgar Allan Poe refreshing the drinks to carry vowels through.

And I think of Sarah Kay dialing tones and sentences you know.

And I think of Bianca Phipps selling secrets and importing pink seashells.

And I think of Patrick Roche listening to wondrous bowels hoping for the win.

And I think of Alice Walker riding the waves of literature.

And I think of Rachel Wiley washing the deep poetry with a tearful smile.

Kasey C. Jones

Take the Lead or Wish to Simply Be

Like Maya Angelou declared, I am gay. I am Lesbian. I am gender non-conforming. I am queer. I am black. I am white. I am Asexual. I am Native American. I am Christian. I am Jewish. I am Muslim. I am Asian. I am Middle Eastern. I am atheist. I am vegan. I am vegetarian. I am an omnivore. I am non-binary. I am it all. I am you. I wish to take the lead, or I wish to simply be.

The Day I Turned Forty

My mind was trying to think of something else besides this fact. I am never fearful of it, but it reminds me of the journey that has gone, and that is coming.

Kasey C. Jones

Nail Polish

Nail polish my trusty comrade. I particularly chose your color, your bottle and your brand. I even suspected your addicting smell and when I need to take you off there is nail polish remover which also has these same attributes. Nail polish your tubular cap today's polish is blue and only on one hand.

An "If" In the Smoke

He has sometimes approached direct
on a note of fire and water, from
Africa, Africa's raindrop
or Africa's distant flame full evolved.
he is not one,
he has brothers and
sisters coughing black,
and now Even white. He has been released
as like fog breathes in the morn', he
has helped new lands so steel looking,
when what he builds is future trees,
in the smoke he is sprawls excess,
In a spacing rising up,
turning Up his chain, with those chained too,
all pray,
the slow sweep of giving Thanks to the
divine strongly holds, a separation
to some screams, some could whisper
in desperate length as students
learn through school by a good teacher,
one who clarifies, they'll conquer
colors so rapid Attempting angles
of
vast depth.

Kasey C. Jones

Champions

I try not to judge but often
I will decide between honey
or jam. I try not to judge
people for shortcomings or
flaws but I do cherish the same
respect from others. I suppose
that I am left-handed, I am naturally
Soft-spoken, I often color outside of
the lines in life which makes me
stand out, but I understand that
we all are champions, small, wide,
old, curved, dim, smart, neat and
giggly.

Intrinsic of Us

Outside lookers see her pacts, they'll stare,
to lost workers wanting nice share,
as shutters close intrinsic of us.
Flashing crass, this nation's head are
my faces, my code rolling past stead receiver,
this scars my satisfaction gear.
there is no glyptic soul's way,
giving lawless experiences,
I am one whole united.
gene of America starves,
grace of America flourishes and glistens,
I'll call last, them who need me.
when only an ear open then
may some blinds: take acceptation,
for my apparent threat be part me.

Kasey C. Jones

The Realest Realness If You Were Gay In the 90s

The unknowing exist, baking white cake,
sheer poison in eyes of great leaders,
in every volume, velocity wheeling,
live iced aces are slack on my side,
using false purity images, and
Chef creates a sense of nurturing.
cognizances push weak politics,
riles mass overlooked by nurturing,
because one way; rule to succeed.
whiz frees authoritative tasks of deed.
CLARITY, ashamed fall those having
perceived darkness common comes, in
variegated nature, or simply
beautiful colors.
our land, comes this
reward to honest voices bleeding.
now listen without rejection and
view your naked idealism.
True practical needs do contest zeal,
so, this flail is worth my while.

Above

I lay my footsteps out, Heart
and Mind for when I must go
see above, deeply irrational people
and strategize a fit ripple addicted,
moving souls better than mine,
and accommodate a strict hand of music,
strategize some good deeds said
to compose you all calm, collected of earth's
sandy colored skin rhythms
by reason, due that I am
just regular people to lay, wake and live
out these hearts; and minds above,
you, so.

Kasey C. Jones

Moves Bull

Red blows my cruise ship sailing,
light moment retires awe,
this urge promoting feeling
of slowed calm, mocking bliss, focus,
and even stimulation.
'm chasing a vacation,
to boot a cut open bruise, where
the arena emits danger.

Flower Beast

I dare dip dahlia in dinner,
these inner organs cringe with bear fear
as acidosis is steep inside me.
that stiff caraway mirrors, my
achiever spinning myth, succeeding.
a dim acacia flaring rare, like, childlike
toys, an old wow, food to white owl
environment, the ultimate
bowl, strong pure care a vow, I make them
people in the land who cherish plants.
expend picture a dramatist since
I'm everywhere, linked to you.
our flowers are clear, older joys,
near tiny trees for supper which
whisk cold wind by those warm, sweet limbs.

Kasey C. Jones

If You Feel Unwell

Know that a glass of water is within reach,
Know that, that tasty bowl of chicken soup is waiting,
Know that both your mom and dad actually loves you
and if they don't there is a substitute out there
somewhere.
Know that your policeman is there to serve,
Know that your doctor is looking out for you,
Know that your teacher has your heart in mind,
Know that your professor will agree to disagree
and if you could just change your thinking
Please know that someone loves you.

Smashing Windows

Inflation, gas prices, grocery store price increases, mass shootings

Kasey C. Jones

Viral Speaking

Turtles, whispers in pink
beginning hatch and crawl
while I move because I
am the dirt learning and
recording this viral speaking,
first words for my parents,
the reason I go on.

Mosaic

One thought, mental attribute are a
mosaic. I've learned that as a kid I was yanked
out of musical harmony and
a heinous world dealt me a bleak hand
to play against everyone else,
such a silly thought prepared with a
side of immaturity.

Kasey C. Jones

Operative Word Blue

Something that color following,
Protecting me possibly my imagination,
or like divine in disguise. I sense that
it's bluish because that color relates to
green (representation of nature) and
relates to purple (representing spirituality).

Yes, it's blue that sits in the middle of my,
hand, of my mind, of my favorite waters.

And when white is unavailable, blue can
Substitute for peace and sky.

Clouds

It sometimes is apparent that the cold clouds
are demanding me but I can't reach those
high standards.

Quite possibly there are periods where I feel
like crying but the joke is on me because
no tears come out.

I compare it to tunnel vision
Yielding nothing more than confinement.

Pine trees hold dew, pine drops
Draw colors of sandy Puke,
Half an hour later the same proves true
traveling through a fungus forest barefoot
would suit musical tunes, brew
and happy songs for malnourished lungs.

It is okay for he or she to tear up
and release facial streams (but prefers
the stream thins).

Mentally Growing

I stepped in the churning light, on
that heated bare back binding,
because, my head fell, and I
quick looked to my palms. I'd pushed
past the floors, I must've invaded any
walls and I stood like a frosted cake
baking away.

Kasey C. Jones

Pasture Robes

The mail is a cold summer mess
and we're moving to and from to
avoid mosquitos yet either
my maroon glasses are melting
or there is water marinating them.

Of course, I am content to be
wearing my pasture robe. It was
gifted to me by the rain and
whistles of the sky, handcrafted
outgo.

They Would Say

I guess they would say that I am
their contact, their child, clear ocean
humming cool waves in their dreams.

I know they would say that I am
Significant and quite royal
And I am assisting you here.

I hope they would say that I am
graceful with an objective closed
and just deciding what's up next.

Kasey C. Jones

Frustrations

As the bear rises in the forest
a violent black
so comes river peering while
dark and green.
I approached my cub heavy
breathing and slurping icy
water and frustration for the
lack of fish meant for dinner time.
The fountain on Forest's river
cut my thirst and then that of baby
cub in like a sporting event
and the frustration soon spoiled.

Babies

Look at the night babies
Translucent and deaf,
Wishing nothing wishes
As if to reap the best.
Some kids do warm and die
For love the only just
That will tend their eyes.
Where the darkness boils
Pass the old lever,
Some children crawl
And lie on water,
No status order
People in the streets.

Kasey C. Jones

People In the Streets

You have the power to change your circumstance.
Believe in yourself and conspire to plan and act.
Do what you feel the cosmos want you to do.
Never give up and remember that you are being guided.
There is no such thing as a wrong direction because
YOU will find your way just remain receptive.

About the Author

At times Kasey opts to focus at varied levels on the sum of his sexuality over the more common topic of skin color; based on his personal experiences. He sees this as his opportunity to effect a change that he envisions for his generation.

Kasey grew up in the 80s and 90s and he is very proud that his voice is from this time period. In Kasey's words, people born in both the 80s and the 90s are a bridge to the future, even though in reality, every generation is in fact, a bridge to the future.

Printed in the United States
by Baker & Taylor Publisher Services